D0461164

NO LONGER PROPERTY OF
MC COUNTY LIBRARY SYSTEM

JUN 2015

Go To Sleep, Maddie!

BY Maureen Wright ILLUSTRATED BY Elisabeth Schlossberg

two lions

KING COUNTY LIBRARY SYSTEM

In loving memory of my friend Joanne Bidlack—M.W.

For Laurent, Claire, and Anna—E.S.

two lions

Text copyright © 2015 by Maureen Wright
Illustrations copyright © 2015 by Elisabeth Schlossberg

All rights reserved. No part of this book may be reproduced, or stored in a retrieval system,
or transmitted in any form or by any means, electronic, mechanical, photocopying, recording,
or otherwise, without express written permission of the publisher.

Published by Two Lions, New York
www.apub.com

Amazon, the Amazon logo, and Two Lions are trademarks of Amazon.com, Inc., or its affiliates.
ISBN-13: 978-1-4778-2627-0
ISBN-10: 1-4778-2627-0
Design by Abby Dening
The artwork was created with soft pastels

Printed in China (R)
First Edition
10 9 8 7 6 5 4 3 2 1

Maddie was all tucked in and ready for bed. There was just one thing....

"I need a drink of water!" said Maddie.
"You already had one," Mommy replied. "It's
time to sleep. Sweet dreams."

"Please read me a story!" said Maddie.
"I've already read you *three* stories," said Daddy.
"Night, night, Maddie."

"It's dark in here!" yelled Maddie.
"The night-light is on," said Mommy. "Now please close your eyes and go to sleep."

"I'm scared of monsters!" said Maddie.
"There's no such thing as monsters," said
Daddy. "But Roofus will keep you company.
Go to sleep, Maddie."
Roofus thumped his tail.

Maddie's parents kissed her one last time and left the room.

"I have to go to the bathroom!" Maddie hollered.

But no one answered. The room was dark
and still, until . . .

“Quackers! Quackers!”

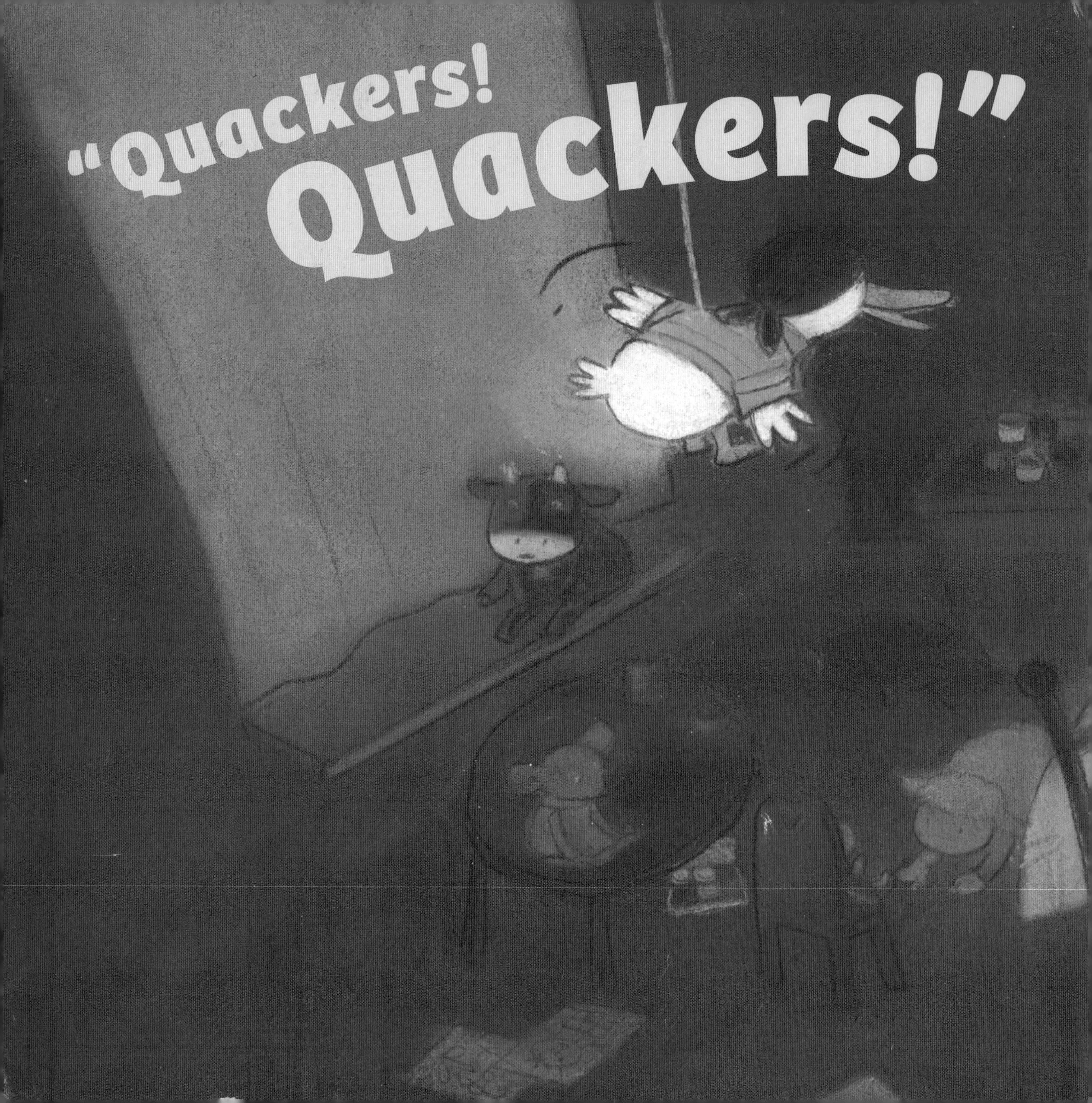

Duck flew down to the bed. "I'm hungry," he said. "I want quackers! Some water, too, please."

Maddie gave him a sip of water. "I don't have any crackers," she said. "Close your eyes and go to sleep."

"R-read it. R-read it."

Frog hopped up on the bed with his favorite book.

Maddie read him the story.

"R-read it again, please," Frog said.

So she read it again. And again.
"R-read it again, please," Frog begged.
"No more," said Maddie. "Go to sleep!"

"Mo-o-o-o-n!"

"Now what?" said Maddie.
"Please open the curtains," said Cow.
"The mo-o-o-o-n is my nightlight."

Maddie opened the curtains. "There," said
Maddie, "now close your eyes." She snuggled
back under the covers.

"Eeeeeek!"

Maddie knew it was her friend Little Mouse.
She peeked under the bed.

"Eeeeeek!" Little Mouse squeaked. "I think
there's a monster under here!"

"There's no such thing as monsters," said Maddie. "But I'll keep you company. There's room in my bed. Hush now. It's time to sleep!"

"Baaaaath-room!"

Sheep jumped up. "I have to go to the baaaaath-room."

Maddie pattered over to the door and opened it for Sheep.

After a minute he returned.
"Okay, climb on up," Maddie said. "Go to sleep!"

"Who? Who?"

Owl landed on Maddie's bed. "WHO is going to kiss us good night?" he asked.

"I will, of course," Maddie said. She gave each of her friends a hug and a kiss. She tucked them in tight. "Night, night, everyone. You, too, Roofus. Now, for the last time . . .

go to sleep!"

And that's just what they did.